A MESSAGE TO PARENTS

Reading good books to young children is a crucial factor in a child's psychological and intellectual development. It promotes a mutually warm and satisfying relationship between parent and child and enhances the child's awareness of the world around him. It stimulates the child's imagination and lays a foundation for the development of the skills necessary to support the critical thinking process. In addition, the parent who reads to his child helps him to build vocabulary and other prerequisite skills for the child's own successful reading.

In order to provide parents and children with books which will do these things, Brown Watson has published this series of small books specially designed for young children. These books are factual, fanciful, humorous, questioning and adventurous. A library acquired in this inexpensive way will provide many hours of pleasurable and profitable reading for parents and children.

Published by Brown Watson (Leicester) Ltd.
ENGLAND
© 1980 Rand McNally & Company
Printed and bound in the German Democratic Republic.

The Owl and
the Pussy-Cat
and Calico Pie

By EDWARD LEAR

Illustrated by Irma Wilde

𝓑𝓻𝓸𝔀𝓷 𝓦𝓪𝓽𝓼𝓸𝓷

England.

THE OWL AND THE PUSSY-CAT

The Owl and the Pussy-Cat went to sea
  In a beautiful pea-green boat:
They took some honey, and plenty of
    money,
  Wrapped up in a five-pound note.

The Owl looked up to the stars above,
And sang to a small guitar,
"Oh, lovely Pussy, Oh, Pussy, my love,

What a beautiful Pussy you are,
                You are,
                You are!
What a beautiful Pussy you are!"

Pussy said to the Owl, "You elegant fowl,
  How charmingly sweet you sing!
Oh! let us be married; too long we have
    tarried:
    But what shall we do for a ring?"

They sailed away, for a year and a day,
  To the land where the bong-tree
    grows;
And there in a wood a Piggy-wig stood,

With a ring at the end of his nose,
His nose,
His nose,
With a ring at the end of his nose.

"Dear Pig, are you willing to sell for one
    shilling
    Your ring?"
Said the Piggy, "I will."

So they took it away, and were married
next day
By the turkey who lives on the hill.

They dined on mince and slices of
  quince,
Which they ate with a runcible spoon;

And hand in hand, on the edge of the sand
They danced by the light of the moon,
The moon,
The moon,
They danced by the light of the moon.

CALICO PIE

Calico Pie,
The little birds fly
Down to the calico-tree:
Their wings were blue,
And they sang "Tilly-loo!"

Till away they flew;
   And they never came back to me!
   They never came back,
   They never came back,
They never came back to me!

Calico jam,
The little Fish swam
Over the Syllabub Sea.

He took off his hat
To the Sole and the Sprat,

And the Willeby-wat:
But he never came back to me;
He never came back,
He never came back,
He never came back to me.

Calico ban,
The little Mice ran
To be ready in time for tea
Flippity flup,
They drank it all up,

And danced in the cup:
But they never came back to me;
They never came back,
They never came back,
They never came back to me.

Calico drum,
The Grasshoppers come,
The Butterfly, Beetle, and Bee,

Over the ground,
Around and round,